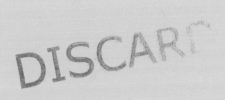

NANUK
THE ICE BEAR

by JEANETTE WINTER

BEACH LANE BOOKS
New York London Toronto Sydney New Delhi

At the top of the world
snow falls . . .

and falls.

Layers of snow freeze into icy glaciers
that cover the bare mountains

and slowly slide down to the sea.

The top of the sea freezes too.

Nanuk, the ice bear,
lives in this quiet white world.

She hunts for food on the sea ice
and in the cold waters.

Great chunks of the glacier break away
and become icebergs that float out to sea.

Nanuk is hungry.

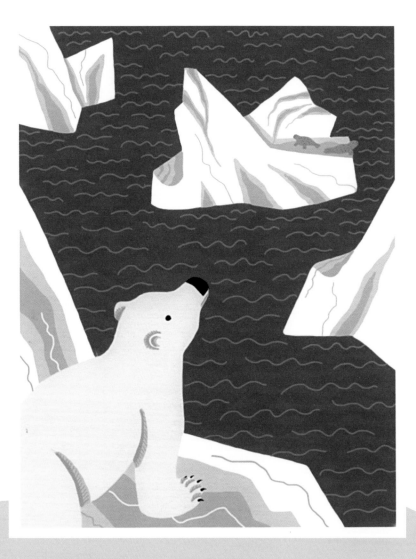

She sees seals in the faraway distance.

She swims closer and looks,

but the seals slide down into the water
and escape.

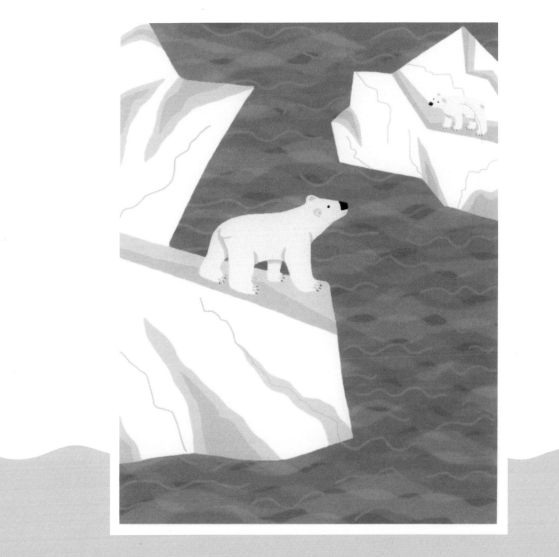

Nanuk sees another ice bear

and swims toward him.

She climbs up high to his perch,

and the two bears dance a dance of courtship.

Later they swim back to the sea ice

to hunt through air holes
seals have made in the ice to breathe.

Days grow shorter.

The two bears sleep in the snow,
warmed by their fur and each other.

When the long night of winter begins,
Nanuk digs alone through the ice and snow
to make her winter den.

She climbs down deep

to the cozy underground hideaway
and waits for her cubs to be born.

Above, in the dark,
ice bears and snow foxes
hunt for food.

And below,
Nanuk welcomes two tiny cubs to her ice world.

She nurses her cubs

and watches them grow
all through the dark Arctic winter.

When the sunlight returns,
her cubs are ready for the world.

Nanuk guides them up to the light

to discover the ice and snow and sunshine.

She teaches her cubs to hunt

and to swim

and to fish.

After two or three summers have passed,
the cubs are ready to go off on their own.

Nanuk watches them leave.

Then she returns to her solitary life.

But the quiet white world is changing.

The ice is melting.
The sea is rising.

Soon there will be no place to hunt.

Nanuk sleeps. She dreams of snow
falling
and falling

and freezing into ice
that slides down to the sea

so once again she can hunt

and raise new cubs

at the top of the world.

For Roger

Further Reading about Polar Bears and Global Warming

Kazlowski, Steven, Theodore Roosevelt IV, et al. *The Last Polar Bear: Facing the Truth of a Warming World*. Seattle, WA: Mountaineers Books, 2008.
———. *Ice Bear: The Arctic World of Polar Bears*. Seattle, WA: Mountaineers Books, 2010.
Stirling, Ian. *Polar Bears: The Natural History of a Threatened Species*. Markham, Ont.: Fitzhenry & Whiteside, 2011.
———. *Polar Bears*. Ann Arbor: University of Michigan Press, 1998.

BEACH LANE BOOKS • An imprint of Simon & Schuster Children's Publishing Division • 1230 Avenue of the Americas, New York, New York 10020 • Copyright © 2016 by Jeanette Winter • All rights reserved, including the right of reproduction in whole or in part in any form. • BEACH LANE BOOKS is a trademark of Simon & Schuster, Inc. • For information about special discounts for bulk purchases, please contact Simon & Schuster Special Sales at 1-866-506-1949 or business@simonandschuster.com. • The Simon & Schuster Speakers Bureau can bring authors to your live event. For more information or to book an event, contact the Simon & Schuster Speakers Bureau at 1-866-248-3049 or visit our website at www.simonspeakers.com. • Book design by Ann Bobco • The text for this book is set in Museo. • Manufactured in China • 1115 SCP • First Edition • 10 9 8 7 6 5 4 3 2 1 • Library of Congress Cataloging-in-Publication Data • Winter, Jeanette, author, illustrator. • Nanuk the ice bear / Jeanette Winter. • pages cm • Summary: At the top of the world, a polar bear hunts, swims, courts, raises cubs, and worries as they go off on their own. • ISBN 978-1-4814-4667-9 (hardback) — ISBN 978-1-4814-4668-6 (eBook) • 1. Polar bear—Juvenile fiction. [1. Polar bear—Fiction. 2. Arctic regions—Fiction.] I. Title. • PZ10.3.W6877Nan 2015 • [E]—dc23 • 2015005169